A RAINBOW OF ODDLY STORIES

SADAKAT ALI

ISBN 979-888555326-1

Contents

Preface

This book is an effort to bring some thrilling experience which bound to happens in this world. They are supernatural happenings which many people have experienced or listened during their life. They are very scary and people who faced them can only know its intensity, while others do not easily believe such happenings. People always make fun of victim's of supernatural happenings. I also do not strongly believe in supernatural activities, but also do not denied them completely. These stories are though work of fiction inspired by true incidents. As I am personally very interested listening to supernatural happenings. They just take us to another world and thrill us, and forced everyone to think hard.

This book is a pure work of fiction and any resemblance to any person living or dead, place or incidence is purely co incidence.

Sadakat Ali (Author)

CHAPTER ONE

HOSPITAL MATRON

Netar Singh was an old man aged 67 years who lived in a beautiful village named Sonawarghat, a village situated in high altitude in hilly area of Himalaya mountain range and nearby town situated near his village was about 45 kilometers from village Sonawarghat namely called Bhadurpur. Netar Singh was a farmers and his family was very big consisting of five brothers and sisters. His family holds a large cultivated land in the village and the families was dependent on and farming and were self reliant. The village was due its location have cold climate throughout the year. The medical facility was not very good in the village due to its remote locality. Netar Singh very hardworking and honest person, he used to help needy whenever anyone need him. He was very cooperative to every villager and as such due to such qualities he was not only well known in his own village but also in the adjoining villages also. He was very fond of eating delicious food and travelling these factors forced him to visit new places also. This needs a lot of time.

It was the year 1968 that during his one of travel he was injured during transit. He had a minor cut in his one of the leg. After reaching his house he just does look traditional bandaging. The wound was just healing in the meantime he starts suffering from influenza. He starts using traditional method of curing influenza, but after 3 to 4 days the condition starts getting bad so he rush to nearby dispensary, where the doctor check him and prescribe medicines. After this he take these medicines for next 3 days but his health starts worse in place getting healed. As a result her family members again took him to the dispensary. The doctor after examining him advised there family members to took him to the Government hospital to the nearby town Bhadurpur. The doctor told the family members of Netar Singh there could be a serious problem so it's better to take him to the Government hospital at this all family members got very afraid , but Doctor said that he would be cured there as all facilities are available in big hospital which are not available here in the dispensary. You therefore take him to the town hospital immediately.

The family members on the advised of the doctor took him to the town hospital on the same evening. Where he was thoroughly checked by doctors and immediately admitted for the treatment. *The next morning seems to be kind on Netar Singh as he feels some improvement in his health and on seeing this family members also got relaxed. The doctor who was on routine ward patients of examination of patients after examination of Netar Singh told the family members that there improvement in his health but we will keep him the hospital for two more days under observation.* The day passed quite well for him, but the night again brings trouble for him and family members. In the late night his health got very worse and the doctor gave some emergency treatment after examining him. The doctor immediately directed the nurses and ward boys to immediately shift him in the isolation ward. On this the family members got very scared and ask the doctor what has happened and why they were shifting him to other ward, the doctor just assured the family members that there is no need to worry we just shifting him for precaution for himself and others.

He also advised the family members that they would not be allowed to meet him during the period of further treatment, but the doctor assured his family members that all facilities and special care will be provide to the patient by hospital during the treatment period. The isolation ward was at a corned place in that hospital. The entry of that ward from another side of the main gate of hospital which was guarded by security personnel's for 24 hours strictly. No one was allowed to enter that restricted path for isolation without prior permissions of authorities, where Netar Singh was shifted for treatment. In the morning all the test of Netar Singh was taken again and a group of doctors came to the conclusion that he was suffering from a deadly virus whose cure is not possible in those days. The doctors also came to a conclusion that Netar Singh would just survive for just another 5 to 7 days. The conclusion of the group of doctors was also communicated to the all family members present in the hospital on that day. They all were shocked and some of them immediately start crying. The group of doctors being human advised the family members to be bold and except the truth. They feel sorry for their patient and also said that they all are feeling helpless and very sad for not providing treatment to Netar Singh. Further the panel of doctors also told them he would be kept in isolation ward.

During this the elder son of Netar Singh named Bachitar Singh asked doctors to allow them to take to their home, the group told him that this virus is very infectious and government have issued guidelines on this to keep the patient in isolation ward if anyone is infected by this as this could result in a pandemic. It is safety of other people that necessary precaution would be taken by the hospital authorities.

This news of the disease spreads like a forest fire not only in the hospital but also in the town also. It becomes a hot topic for discussion in the town. Who ever heard about this got scared. These result in that no staff of that hospital agreed to attend the patient in the isolation ward. Even the doctor who was in charge of Netar Singh goes on leave. In the next morning the family members of Netar Singh except his elder son Bachitar Singh went back to their village. At this juncture a Old man who was a part of security team of that hospital and used to perfumed duties on the main gate of that hospital named Brij Lal between 8 PM to 8 AM starts just starts keeping food in front of the isolation word from that day onwards. Some other members of hospital staff advised him not to do so.

But the old man just ignored them and tells everyone that the patient is no doubt suffering from dreadful disease but he would need food till he is alive and he cannot stop as such. Bachitar Singh elder son starts staying in the Gurdwara and from that day he was just anticipating of bad news at any moment. The mind stage of him cannot be described in words as he was also not allowed to even see his father. The days goes passing by and on the eight day of the doctor who was on leave arrived in the hospital and first thing he do was to inquire from the support staff about Netar Singh. The staff told him that no one has visited that isolation ward from the day Netar Singh was shifted in that ward. After knowing this the doctor immediately called the meeting of hospital administration on the issue and in the meeting it was decided to sent a team of staff to check and bring the body of Netar Singh and hand over to the family after taking all necessary steps as laid down in the government guidelines issue. So the team was send to that ward and after 15 minutes some members of that team just came running to the doctor and said to the doctor that the patient is alive and looks perfectly alright. After hearing this doctor was just shocked and angrily replied stop joking.

But the member of support staff they were not joking and the situation is not such that anyone would dare to do that. The doctor on realizing this directed the staff members to follow him. After reaching the ward and on seeing that Netar Singh is alive and looks fine the word which came out from doctor mouth was – How it is possible? And after a while and gathering himself the doctor ask Netar Singh how is feeling now. Netar Singh replied – He is Fine. On this juncture the doctor after thinking for a while, directed the support staff to take the patient for all medical test immediately and provide him all the reports within one hour. In between he also asks a staff member about any family member of patient is nearby, and ask to call him. The staff on this said to doctor that the patient elder son is staying the Nearby Gurdhawara form the very first day. The staff immediately rushed to the cal the elder son of Netar Singh. When Bachitar Singh came to knew from staff member that his father is alright and the doctor had called him, His son was just shocked and starts crying and immediately run towards hospital.

Bachitar Singh after reaching the doctor room and seeing his father was sitting alive; he just cannot control himself and hug his father immediately. During this one of the staff bring the latest medical reports of Netar Singh and over the doctor. The doctor took a while and goes through those reports and found that everything was perfectly alright. After this the doctor asks Netar Singh whether he has any medicines during his isolation period. Who use to attend him during this period? He said he used to find meal kept outside the door of ward and a matron use to visit the ward every night between 12 AM to 12.30 AM. She uses to give some medicines and injection every day. After a while Bachitar Singh asks doctor – If my father is alright, in that case could he take father back home. On this doctor reply- That they would keep his father under medical observation for next 24 hours after that he would be discharged. This news of Netar Singh also makes headlines in the hospital and town from that time onwards. But the doctor did not still believe what he had noticed. The doctor immediately calls upon two matrons of the hospital and who among them have attended Netar Singh during the isolation period.

But both of the matron denied the query put before them by doctor. On this doctor calls Netar Singh and ask him to identify the matron who has attended him. Netar Singh after seeing both matrons replied the matron who attended him not present here. After that the doctor calls all staff members and even security personnel and put same question before them, but everyone denied the query. This makes doctor more shocked and at this stage he was not getting any clue about the scenario and as a result he was getting very anxious too. The next day Netar Singh was discharged from the hospital, as he was leaving the hospital with his elder son the doctor also accompany them to way leading to the main exit gate. On the way leading to the gate and on the walls near isolation ward of that hospital some photographs of event happened in that hospital was hanging. During their walking Netar Singh ask the doctor to see one of the pictures hanging on the wall and said and pointed out to a picture and said that this was the matron who use to attend him in isolation ward. After that the Netar Singh and his son leave the hospital.

The doctor came back to his room and calls one of the senior members of the staff. He took him the place where a picture was hanging and explained everything to his staff member. On this that staff member said – it is not possible doctor the matron whom Netar Singh has identified had expired before 8 to 9 years ago. He leaves the place just saying that Netar Singh may be just mistakenly identify the picture. The doctor again return back to his room and now his surprise about Netar Singh took a new height and made him more venerable at this moment. The days pass by and the said doctor has no answer to his question.

After a week the old security man Brij Lal who used to keep meal outside the room of isolation ward for Netar Singh and was on leave , visited the doctor in the morning in his room and tell doctor that he had listen everything from staff members about Netar Singh and wants to tell something about it. He also requested the doctor to believe him and not get annoyed with him. The doctor immediately asks him to tell what he knew about Netar Singh. He said that the matron which Netar Singh identified was ROZA; she was employee of this hospital.

She was an extra ordinary lady and very hardworking. She used to even work for 24 hours when ever needed to do so. On this doctor said that the other employee of the hospital had told him that she had died some 8 to 9 years ago. On this Brij Lal told that it's true, doctor as you have been working in this hospital for last 3 years as such you would not be aware of the story of matron ROZA. It was a chilly night of winter of December some 9 years ago when she was on night duty. Then duty room at that time was the same room which is now isolation ward at present. On that night around 12.15 AM the matron after attending the entire patient goes back to his duty room and seat on the chair near a room near a room heater. She was wearing siphon sari on that night. Soon she fell asleep and after sometime the hospital listens the shouting of matron for help. The whole staff present and even some patient ran towards the duty room. I was also present on duty that night. As we all reaches the duty we all saw that the sari of matron had caught fire. On seeing this we put off the fire after a while. The staff took the matron to the ward for treatment. But the matron had more than 80 percent burns due to that fire.

All best medical was provided to the matron but after 2 days the matron died. On listening to this the doctor asks Brij Lal if all this had happened in past, than how it is possible that Netar Singh experience. On this Brij Lal again requested to doctor that which he would tell now about that matron is very supernatural and very hard to believe. In the past many patient who were admitted in isolation ward and were cases which bound not to survive got cured. But one thing common in them were that they all wants to thanks a particular matron for services. Some of them even met het matrons of the hospital, who were employed in the hospital and never found that matron who served them. I and some of the other staff know about this. I usually performed night duty and one night I noticed that a matron was going in isolation ward I follow her. But she quickly entered the door of the ward entrance. When I reach the corridor the ward, I was shocked to notice that no one was there walking in the corridor. I further may every possible inquiry about this incidence. This whole incidence makes me scared for several days thereafter. Than after some days when a patient identify matron ROZA in the same picture while leaving the hospital, which makes me more scared about the incidence which I faced that night.

I got confirmation of my fear some few years ago. On that I was as usual performing my night duty and around 12.10 AM a matron entered the gate and goes towards isolation ward. The matron gives me resemblance to matron ROZA, but I just not bothered at that moment as there some emergencies cases have arrived on that night. But in the evening I made an inquiry about any new matron had joined the hospital, but making all my sincere efforts about this for several days I got no reply from any staff and administration side. After that as time passes by and some other such happening going around from several years I came to perception that the spirit of matron ROZA still resides in this hospital , which does not haunt anybody instead just cures people by what methods Almighty better knows. *The spirit of matron ROZA is very helpful and it just behaves like the matron when she was alive. Brij Lal further told doctor that it is a paranormal incidence which is hard to believe and explain. But the recent example of Netar Singh and its treatment as explained by patient who got cured against all odds just confirmed me about the spirit of matron ROZA. I do believe in this and as such I shall always rembered matron ROZA for rest of my life.*

After listening to Brij Lal about the tragedy which was faced by matron ROZA and knowing everything about her dedication towards duties. Moreover about the some of the happening over the years the doctor becomes speechless.

On this Brij Lal leaves the doctor room without further exchanging any word with doctor. After that the doctor sits silently for next couple of hours on his chair on that day. The doctor got so confused about this on that moment. He was not able to decide whether to listen to the voice of mind or heart.

But the said doctor still rembered the whole incident regarding Netar Singh which he had witnessed in that hospital. He is not sure whether to believe that or not. The thin line between supernatural incidence and truth still haunts him But one thing he still rembered each and every word of Brij Lal which he told him about matron ROZA.

CHAPTER TWO

HOSTEL BOY

Mahesh and Nikhil were two very close friends who were resident of a beautiful village of named SONWARGHAT. They were neighbors and belong to same age group. From the early age they both enjoy company of each other and shares many common likes and dislikes. In that village the only centre for studies was a government school and as such they both went to the same school for their respective education. In those days the game was very popular and them facility of this game was also available in that school also. They both start playing hockey from the early age. In the few years they both becomes very good players of hockey and were selected in school team to participate in inter school championship. There school starts winning the inter school championships from the arrival of both in the team. The commitment of both for hockey soon becomes their passion with the passé of time. They want to do something special in the field hockey not only for their school, district, and state but for the country. As a result after completing their school studies they both decided to move to nearby town of Bhadurpur for higher studies and hockey.

They both convinced their parents who also back them during their schooling of playing hockey. In the town there were all facilities for the sports. They were very hard working in every aspect of their life. Whether it is studies, sports or even in every household activities. These qualities help them to get all support from their respective families to move to town in search of their aim. They both got admitted to the same government college and got accommodation in a hostel situated at the outskirts of the town. And in their college every facility for hockey was available which make them both happy and satisfying. The quality of education of that college was also very high which just mad them more committed for fulfilling their dreams. The hostel in which they got accommodation was situated at a distance of 1.5 kms from the town at a hilltop. A natural waste sewerage separates the hostel from the town and around that there was dense jungle. Every facility of food, entertainment and medical were available in the town for the hostel occupants, though some basic amenities were provided to the occupants of hostel by the hostel authorities.

As such every occupants of that hostel used to visit the town daily for their some requirements. But some occupants returned to the hostel late after watching late night movies. Mahesh and Nikhil also use to practice this sometime and both returns to the hostel late in the night on many occasions after watching late night movies in the cinema hall. In the hostel they both got adjoining rooms. Their studies and sports were going very well with the passage of time. They were acclaimed by college administration for their commitment towards both towards studies and sports.

The time passage by and it was the second year of their college during which the father of Nikhil expired. As a result he has to go his native village for nearly 2 months. When after spending nearly 2 months in the village Nikhil returns to his college. And when he met Mahesh , he was very shocked to notice that he has looking very weak and some occupants of the hostel also tell Nikhil for quite some time he is not playing hockey and even skipping college classes also. This makes Nikhil very worried from Mahesh side.

On that day Nikhil just went to his room and starts continuing his studies from the next day. From that day onwards one thing Nikhil noticed and feel that Mahesh is always keeps on avoiding him. When he asks Mahesh after a couple of days, Why is he avoiding him , what wrong he had committed and what factors are making this happen in their childhood friendship. Mahesh just said – nothing doing on his part and nor he avoiding him. It's just your imagination. They both had this conversation at the dinner table that day. After that they went back to their respective rooms. The days starts on passing by , during which Nikhil noticed that Mahesh was getting weaker and weaker with passage of time.

After 20 days Mahesh fell ill and Nikhil took him to the hospital where doctor thoroughly examine Mahesh and prescribed him the medicines. He further advised Mahesh not to take any stress of any kind. On this Nikhil asks doctor, whether something serious on which doctor tell that the reports does show anything serious, but it seems he is taking some stress of something. But doesn't worry give him the medicines on time and he would be fine soon. After that they both returned to the hostel.

From that day onward Nikhil starts taking full care of Mahesh and act according to the advised given the doctor. He also advised and guides Mahesh not to take any stress of any kind. If there is any problem please tell him and he will solve it. But Mahesh use to always deny of having any problem. During this period when ever Nikhil got break he starts asking about any particular event happened with Mahesh during his absence from the hostel. The other occupants denied the very inquiry made by Nikhil. As such he doesn't get any clue from anybody about Mahesh taking stress. Nikhil was taking every possible care of Mahesh, but as days were passing by the health of Mahesh was getting worse. So after seeing his health, Nikhil again took him to the hospital on 8th day from when his treatment begins. The doctor in the hospital on seeing the condition of Mahesh was surprised. He re-examine him and took all other medical tests again. All medical test of Mahesh was perfectly alright. The doctor again advised Mahesh not to take any stress of any kind and changed the medicines for further treatment. They both returned to their hostel again.

After seeing the health of Mahesh, Nikhil called mother and father of Mahesh to the hostel. The mother and father of Mahesh reached the hostel on the same evening. In the next morning a person named Bhahadur Singh who used to deliver morning tea and snacks to the occupants of that hostel approaches Nikhil. He told Nikhil that as he noticing that Mahesh health is getting worse day by day in spite of taking treatment on regular basis. I think he is not suffering from any disease, but he had become a victim of some supernatural activity. Such type of incidents has also reported to happen in adjoining area in the past. Nikhil after listening to all this had no word to speak. He does not believe in any type of supernatural happenings. The mother and father of Mahesh were very scared of the condition of Mahesh. In the same night Nikhil told to the mother of Mahesh about Bhahadur Singh and also narrates everything told by him. On this his mother said to Nikhil that you're both are child, but son I have listened to many supernatural activities happening with people during my life. I cannot say whether it would be true or not, but no one can deny such things totally. On that night Nikhil wants to stay with Mahesh in anticipation to get any clue from Mahesh.

On that night Nikhil firstly started with words why he does not allow him to stay in night during his illness. Tell me everything for sake of your old and poor mother and father. After listening to this Mahesh Starts weeping and on this Nikhil hugs him and again requested to tell his problem.

Mahesh than stated to tell Nikhil something dangerous is happening with him form the last 2 and half months. It all started on the couple of night before you had to go to village due to your father demise. One night I was coming back from town, late in the night after watching a movie. On the way back near the jungle I heard sound of someone weeping behind a tree, on listening to the sound at that time firstly I got scared. But after awhile I think that I must ensure that someone might be in trouble and needs help. So I cautiously follow the sound. When I reach a big tree, there was very beautiful lady weeping behind that tree. I was surprised to see that a lady is weeping in the jungle at this time. Firstly I was very afraid of the situation, but after controlling my emotions I go near to that lady and ask why she is weeping and where she is. I also asks her about the place where she belongs. She took a while before speaking anything. Then she told him that she cannot tell anything at this moment. But she will be very thankful to him, if he could provide shelter for her that night.

After listening to this I told her everything about myself and said he cannot provide shelter to her. But on this she holds my hand and pleaded for help, on which I got very emotional. And I took a while and starts thinking for some possibilities to help that lady. My aim at that moment was to just help the lady. So an idea came in my mind and I said to lady he will take to his room but she had to climb the wall of my room by hanging from a bed sheet rope. As such I took her to my room as discussed between us. After reaching my room she starts thanking me and directed me to sleep on the bed. She further said to me that she will sit in the corner of room and shall exit the room before sunrise. So I just sleep on the bed and the lady sit in the corner. In the middle of night my sleep broke and I was surprised to found that the lady had left the room without intimating me. Next whole day I just keep thinking about this for every single moment. But when was I was verge of going to sleep in night I heard a sound from the window side. I stood up and was surprised to see that the same lady was climbing the wall of my room. She handed her hand to me and asks me to pull her. When she reached my room she just hug me and thanks me for last night.

The first question I asked about her exit from my room in the previous night. She starts explaining to me, that she does not want anybody to see her and also does not want that nobody should blame him. In that night the lady stay in his room and they both have sex between them on that night. In between I want to know her problem, but she just smiles and asks me to leave it. And from that day the lady always visited my room and both have sex ever night. But she never tells anything about herself. I have also tried to know everything about her, for which I use to ask residents of nearby area. But nothing had been heard about that lady. This was the reason why I do not allow you to stay in my room. So I today plead you not to stay in my room. After listening to all things Nikhil went to his room, but he was not able to sleep whole night. He was just thinking about that lady and also tries to think some remedy for the situation which Mahesh was facing. At this moment the name of Bhahadur Singh came into his mind. So he started to wait for the sunrise so that he can meet Bhahadur Singh.

In the morning when Bhahadur Singh arrived in the hostel Nikhil at once took him to his room and tell everything about Mahesh. He further asks him whether such lady resides nearby. On this whole thing Bhahadur Singh tells Nikhil that he is very much sure now that Mahesh is victim of supernatural activity. He further added that only one person name BABA KHAN help them in overcoming this. Baba Khan resides in the town and very famous for his treatment of supernatural's.

They both decided to go to the town at once and meet BABA KHAN. After 2 hours they reach the place of BABA KHAN. When they tell everything to him about Mahesh, The BABA KHAN tells them after doing some spiritual activity. That Mahesh had become a victim of a very dangerous supernatural activity, after listening to this both starts pleading to him to help them to overcome the present crisis. So he gives them a ball of thread and instructed them to first perused Mahesh to just tie that thread end to the hair of that lady. But during doing this care should be taken that lady should got aware of this. He should carry the routine of his meeting with that lady as usual. And he would the place in the next morning. He further directed them to meet him in the jungle.

After that they both return to the hostel and met Mahesh in the room. They told everything which BABA KHAN told them. They both pleaded to act according to direction of BABA KHAN for the sake of his old parents. The night dawn and with grace of Almighty Mahesh Successfully tie the knot of thread in the hair of that lady without any mistake as directed by BABA KHAN. And as promised by BABA KHAN he came early in the morning and met Nikhil and Bhahadur Singh in the jungle. He asks both of them to search the end of the thread. So they both start searching for the same. He further tell them that he had called them in this jungle as no one should get any information about this, Which can make other occupants of the hostel and adjoining area scared. And after some 30 minutes Bhahadur Singh sees the end of that thread in the east direction of the jungle. He immediately pointed it to BABA KHAN who cautioned them not to touch it. They all follow the thread and Nikhil and Bhahadur Singh were amazed to see that the thread end was tied to a human bone lying deep in the jungle. They asks BABA KHAN what they are seeing is hard to believe and requested him to tell about this.

On their query BABA KHAN told them this is bone of lady who have died many years ago, but her rituals as per her religion was not performed accordingly. As such her spirit is forced to just keep on wandering in the jungle. She could be having some relation with the adjoining areas of this jungle. Her wishes were not fulfilled and she died in a young age too. After telling this to them BABA KHAN encircle the area where they have found that bone lying. He further directed Nikhil to dig a deep hole in the ground. It took around 1 hour for them to dig a hole in the ground as desired by BABA KHAN. And when the hole was ready

BABA KHAN said to them to stand away from that place and came here when he ask them to do so. Then he took the bone and tied whole thread round it and throws it in the deep hole dug by Nikhil and Bhahadur Singh. After this he called both of them and asks them to fill the hole with mud.

And after completing the whole process of burin the bone under a deep hole in the earth BABA KHAN directed them to go back to hostel and took oath from them both not tell anything about this, even to Mahesh or his family members. And from that evening Mahesh said to Nikhil that he now feeling better after a long time. This makes Nikhil very satisfying.

The next afternoon the mother of Mahesh told Nikhil the health of Mahesh is getting stable now and they are thinking to take their son to village for some days. And Mahesh is also willing to go to the village. So they all went to the village in the next morning. Nikhil was happy for Mahesh and keeps on thanking Almighty for his grace.

But after a month has just passed by, on one evening a bad news arrived in the hostel regarding Mahesh that he is no more. He died mysteriously in the village in the morning. Which was shocking for Nikhil and Bhahadur Singh? At this moment many questions came in their minds and they both decided to immediately visit BABA KHAN and know the reason behind the untimely demise of Mahesh. As such they both start their journey towards town. They reached the place of BABA KHAN in 2 hours. When they arrive at the place BABA KAHAN asks them to wait for sometime as he was performing some urgent rituals. After 15 minutes BABA KHAN asks both of them to follow him in the nearby room where they could sit and have a detailed conversation. They all reach the room as destined by BABA KHAN and he asks them to sit on the mat.

Before any one of them was able to utter word , BABA KHAN tell them they both have came here to know why Mahesh had died in spite his treatment. On listening this they both were surprised how BABA KHAN knows about their mind thinking. He said everything is in the hand of Almighty and he governs this whole universe. I am just a human and just tried to save Mahesh. He further added that in spiritual world there is a time limit for treatment of any problem. And he was aware of that something like this could happen. But like a doctor it is his duty to try to cure the victims. In case of Mahesh the unseen time limit of treatment had already expired when they approach him. But they all made their best efforts for Mahesh. At least their efforts are not all gone in vain as they now could be sure that that sprit will not be able to make anyone victim like Mahesh in future.

After listening to this they took permission to leave from BABA KHAN and returned back to the hostel thinking about each and every second of their efforts in pursuit of saving Mahesh and thinking they would rembered this for rest of their life.

CHAPTER THREE

A CYCLE RIDER

College life is known as one of the most memorable years of one's life. It is entirely different from school life. College life exposes us to new experiences and things that we are not familiar with earlier. For some people college life means enjoying life to the fullest and partying hard. While for others, it is time to get serious about their career and study thoroughly for a brighter future. The college life is very happy and unforgettable experience in the life of many students. There are huge benefits of college life apart from getting education. Thus college life is quite important. It teaches you the tough skills of life- discipline, friendship, sicereity, dedication, struggle, experiences, joy and commitment. The college life is sweet and wonderful indeed.

I Pinky after school took admission in government college of Bhadurpur for higher studies. When the first year studies started, it marks a new beginning in my life. And every day of college seems to bring new experience for me. Here I met student coming from different places, and have studied in different schools and have grown up in different cultures.

I met many students studying my class and college block. After a month time I met a Student name Amar who was not studying in my block but in the other block of the college, which was situated at distance from my block. But we both met in the college play ground first time. He belongs to village. He was very intelligent and dynamic in every field of college life whether it is studies, sports, cultural activities or social services. These qualities of Amar start impressing me. In no time we both just become friend and starts enjoying each other company. We often go to watch movies in theatre also.

But in the month of November that year he did not met for nearly twenty days, which makes me very eager to know where he is. His college block was situated at distance from my block; he neither met during last twenty days either on way to college nor met me the playground. For the first few days from the last meeting I think that he might have gone to his village. But it had been twenty days after the last meeting and moreover the term one exams had also started which makes me more anxious about Amar. But slowly and steadily one and a half month passed by, my emotions forced me to make sincere efforts to know more about Amar. So one day I decide to visit his block.

I reach the block where he studies inquired from many students about him , all of them gave same reply that they have not seen Amar from nearly one and half month. Due to this my eagerness sores new height and just in stage of shock what that what would happened and why Amar have attended the college. I was also more anxious as I did not know his friends who could at least tell name of his village. In this quest after thinking for a while, decided to go to college office in a hope of getting some information about him.

When I reach the office I approach a clerk who was my neighbour and requested him to tell something about Amar. After listening to my request immediately said that boy Amar had leaved the college. Last week his parents came here and take away his college leaving certificate and character certificate. On this I further ask that office clerk whether he can tell me anything why Amar had leaved the college. The clerk said he knew nothing about his exit from college. But he said to me - I think he must have decided to do some vocational studies.

After listening to all this, I did not get satisfied and slowly starts walking towards my home on that day. But for another couple of days I keeps thinking whole day along about Amar, why he had left the college. The time goes passing by and it took no time the occasion of getting degree appears. But during this passage of time the memories of Amar seems to haunt me sometimes. Now I have started to appear in many competitive examinations for getting employment if governments sector as it was need of hour for me and family. For which these tests centers were located at different places.

During this period once I had to appear in a competitive examination schedule to be held at Shimla. This test was conducting after nearly two years of my completion of college studies. I reach Shimla a day before the examination as my native place was at a very distance place. I took a hotel for night stay on that day. In the evening on that day I was coming back to hotel after having dinner and on the way back I show Amar sitting on a bench on the Mall road, I was so amazed on that moment and quickly approached him. On seeing me Amar just hugs me in the joy again and again.

We both thanks Almighty at that moment for meeting again after nearly five years. After controlling our emotions we first decided to have coffee and then sit on the bench on which he was sitting. So we took coffee from the nearby café and sits on the bench. As we sits on the bench, I immediately asks him – why he left the college without meeting him. On this he said we may have some other discussion first. But on this I said I have been waiting for this moment for last five years. But after thinking for a while Amar replied that your reaction is quite natural. But believe me I did not leave the college due to any normal circumstances. On listening this I got anxious.

I immediately ask Amar not to make any delay in telling the truth. Amar thus started to tell everything about his unprecedented exit from college from Bhadurpur College about five years ago. It was a quite good day for me when I become victim of a supernatural happening. As you must be aware I used reside in college hostel which was situated at the outskirts of the town. The old jail of British was made boys hostel. On that evening I went to see a movie in cinema hall. It was a late night movie and the show of that movie got off around 12AM on that day. After that I exit the cinema hall and started walking towards my hostel. It was nearly three kilometers for me to be covered for reaching the hostel.

On that I was little bit scared about supernatural happening reported to happen between the distance from court complex leading to our hostel. On many occasions I past that way in the night and never get scared about all rumors, which goes around. When on that day nearing the court complex I realize that a cycle is coming from behind. At that point I just think that it would be very nice if that cycle rider give me lift and I will reach hostel very soon. So

I give a signal to that cycle rider for lift and he stops the cycle at distance about three feet from my position at that time.

I immediately rode at the backsheet of the cycle and the cycle rider stated paddling it again it starts moving forward. During this short journey I tried many times to spoke with rider, but he did not utter any word. After a while I sat quietly. And when we reach appoint of diversion from where my way for college hostel bifurcated from the main road, I requested the rider to stop the cycle and drop me there. The rider immediately stops the cycle and I get down from the cycle. I thank the rider for lift but he neither see me nor utter any word from his mouth. But instead he starts paddling the cycle.

As the cycle had just moved about 15 meters forward I just look back and at that moment the cycle rider also seems to rotating his neck. But the horrible thing about his rotating his neck was that the rotation was about 360 degree and his face was very ugly and scary. It was evil spirit and on seeing this I just jump over a stone and starts shouting and running towards the hostel. It was just horrible sight on that moment and it still haunts me in spite of passage of time. I cannot describe in words to you the stage of my mind at that juncture.

After running and shouting for nearly 7 minutes I reach the hostel and on listening to my shouting al occupants of the hostel on that night wake up and came out in the ground. The security guard present on that day just stops me running and immediately asks me what happened. He noticed blood on my paint and shirt as I tumble down many times during my running towards the hostel and got wounded. But at that moment my breathing was very high and as such could able to utter any word from my mouth.

On noticing this warden of hostel gave me a glass of water and asks me to first sit down and relax.

After sometime I was able to control my emotions and explained everything happened with me to the warden, which was anxiously heard by the other occupants of the hostel present at that time. At that moment I decided to leave the hostel and go to my village as soon as possible. The warden first gave first aid to me and on seeing my condition he advised that it would be better to wait for sunrise. On that the reaming nights I was not able to sleep and also requested some student not sleep and sit alongside him.

As the first sight of sunrise in the morning I took my luggage and requested the hostel warden to arrange some vehicle which can drop him at bus stop. Thus I leave the town in the early morning but when the vehicle was crossing the way stretch where the whole incident started and ended, I was just scared during that time period.

After listening this I become speechless for next few minutes. Than we both decided to go the hostel room and meet in the morning. The examination centre for both was same. So we both met in the venue and have breakfast together and go in our respective allotted rooms for test. And around 3 PM the test was over and we both took taxi from the venue for dropping us at bus station.

There we rode in our respective bus which leads to our respective destination. But the departure we exchanged our telephone numbers for having conversation occasionally. I also requested Amar to visit my house sometime – but he just denied that and said ,the supernatural incident would haunt him for rest of his life and as such it cannot possible for him to visit Bhadurpur forever. Instead he requested me to visit his village. For which I shook my head at that time.

After a while the bus of Amar stated to move forward and keeps on watching the bus till it exit my eye sight. My journey on that day towards my home was very emotional, during which I just keeps thinking about Amar encountering that supernatural happening. But after reaching home I just have my dinner quickly and lay down in my bed thinking that today meeting with Amar seems to be a medicine for my wound which resides within my heart and mind for last five years. At this moment the feeling of losing a friend for ever just melts away from my heart.

CHAPTER FOUR

A TREASURY HUNT

Suraj was the only son of a farmer named Dalip Singh. Suraj was the only son in the family which consists of six members. He was quite good in studies and sports. And he always dreams of joining army, but his father always opposes this. They use to have heated conversation between them occasionally on this issue. But despite Suraj never seems to be dropping his dream of becoming an army man. He son some appears in some recruitment tests of army with his cleverness without giving any hint to his family. One day Suraj goes for army test to be held in Bhadurpur. His father had gone to a relative marriage to a distant village. He had not even told to any family members about that army test. Even his mother got at the time, when he took his luggage bag and was about to leave. At this moment his mother just cautioned him that his father will get annoyed when came to know this.

On this Suraj requested his mother you may not tell anything about this to father. He is scheduled to return home after three days, but I will return home next day, even before father return from the marriage and he further requested his mother that he just wants to appear in the test. And appearing in test does not mean that he would definitely join the army. This would help him in other test also as his appearance in test will boast his confidence. But father does not listen to my feelings regarding tests. He then took formal permission from his mother and leaves the home for his journey.

The next day in the evening returned to his home. After a while his mother asks Suraj where his father is. On this Suraj surprisingly said to his mother- Father, what are saying? Have you forget that he may return tomorrow from marriage. On this his mother told him that his father returned home in the afternoon yesterday. The first thing asks me about you. Firstly I just went of ignoring it, but when he got annoyed, than I have to tell whole thing to him. After knowing this he immediately decided to go to town not stop you from appearing in the test, but they really loves you.

I knew they get annoyed very early as he really worries about you. Does he not meet his father in the town, on this he replied –No.? This discussion between family results in building of tension among about Dalip Singh. They all decide to wait till tomorrow afternoon. In the morning after knowing about Dalip Singh not returning with his son forced some neighbors' to visit Suraj Home know more about it. All visitors gave a assurance that he may return today. The just passes by not only whole family but also many neighbors' were keeping close eye on all vehicles which was going and coming on the road of their village. It was nearing evening on that day when some elderly neighbors' gathered in the house, after the last bus had arrived on that date. At this point the whole family got more anxious about Dalip Singh. The elderly people who were gathered at that time suggest the family that Suraj along with some other people may leave early in the morning in search of Dalip Singh. As they were finalizing the next day programs a policemen along with village pardhan reaches the house. On seeing this Suraj mother starts weeping before any one utter a word from his mouth.

This draws attention of all the people gathered in house on that moment. On seeing this village pardhan immediately starts telling to that nothing is serious about Dalip Singh. This policeman has come from the town with a message. First listen to him. The policemen said that Dalip is fine; he just met a accident in the town and is being hospitalized for treatment. On this the whole starts crying. But policemen told them he himself had met Dalip Singh in this morning and please trust him that he just fine. He himself had requested us to deliver this message to the family. After listening to this Suraj mother said that she wants to go to town immediately, to see what had happened to her husband. She cannot trust the words of policemen. After seeing the emotions of family the policemen said – Okay, you all can accompany me in police van. So, all the family members accompany the policemen in van for there journey to the town. They all reach the hospital on the same night and after seeing that Dalip was lying on the bed with bandage on one leg. Though got a little relaxed, but all members at once hug Dalip Singh and starts crying again.

On this Dalip Singh asks every family member to calm down, there is nothing serious issue. Suraj mother immediately ask him to tell everything what and how this happened. On this Dalip Singh starts narrating everything to his family. He started with words that he reaches the town around 9 PM on the same day. He immediately visited three hotels in search of Suraj. But he does not find any clue on that time. So he decided to meet Suraj in the morning in the ground where the test was scheduled to be conducted. After that he decided to find some accommodation for himself and as such visited many hotels and guest houses. But he does not find any accommodation for himself as all places were overcrowded due to army test on that day. So he sits in ground thinking what to do. In that ground two people who were drunkard approaches him and inquired is there any problem. Firstly I hesitate to tell anything to them. But when they again offer me help, on that moment I just tell them he searching for some accommodation. I further requested then to tell some place where he could find accommodation.

On his query they said that they guided me to go along with the adjoining road and after walking for nearly one kilometer he would show a big building on his left hand side on hilltop. That is a big hotel and every can get accommodation at any time. After a while they both leave the place and I started to my walk on that road. And after walking for nearly one kilometer I show a big building on my left hand side. On that moment I feel very relaxed and was thanking both of them in my heart for telling the right way for accommodation. On the side of the road and in the opposite side of the path leading to that building there was a big stone. I just think to relax a bit by way of sitting on the stone for some time and smoke a cigarette. As I watch puffing the cigarette, I realize that someone is sitting on a tomb just behind me. On this I just think that he may be also like me. So I try to have a conversation with him. But in spite I saying something it seems that he does not understand anything. So I become silent, but after sometime when I was standing back and about take my path to the said hotel, I noticed that he is now trying to see me. And when he starts lifting his head a awkward sound listened to me.

And finally when I saw show his face which was very ugly I just ran towards a nearby path. I also realized that the place where he was sitting was a graveyard. This creates more fear in me. After running for a while I show some light of building. So, with all my power I starts running towards those light. During my run I heard some more sounds but I cannot understand them at that moment. Then suddenly a bullet struck my leg and I fell down. Some people took me to a room and then I realize in the lights that they were policemen and the building was state treasury. The policemen asks me who I am and why did not he stops in spite of three cautioned. On this I told each and everything to them. After listening to my story one of the policemen told me both people whom he met in the ground would be crazy. There is no hotel or guest house in this surrounding. The building which designate as hotel is court complex. One of the senior policemen said that he very lucky that he just escaped from that scenario as it is a haunted area and in past many supernatural incidences have been reported to happen at that place. They all feel sorry for me at that moment and further promised to help me. They gave first aid to me and also gave me medicines too. But at time my leg was bleeding a lot.

After that they bring me to this hospital and hospitalized here for my treatment. In the morning the Assistant commissioner of police visited the hospital and asked everything from me. I again narrate each and everything to the ACP. After hearing to my whole story, he feels sorry on behalf of all policemen who were present on that night for patrolling of state treasury. He further conveyed to me that all expenses of my treatment will be borne by the department. I just said to him that there is no need of this. But he just starts requesting me for this. Then I request him to communicate my message of being hospitalized to my family who in village would **worry** a lot for me. He immediately ordered on the spot to a subordinate to immeietely take address my village and send messenger at once. He said to me that I can call me at time if there is need for his presence. Moreover he had posted policemen in ward to take proper care of me and regularly gave him the follow after every two hours. He is a very nice and noble officer.

After carefully listening the narration of father about the whole incident, Suraj starts crying again and hug his father immediately and feels sorry that he is sole responsible for what he have to faced. But on this Dalip Singh hug him tightly for a while and said to him that no you're not responsible for all this. Look at the positive thing in this. Suraj ask his father – what? Dalip Singh said this whole incident have forced us both come close to each other. After listening to this both keeps on hugging each for next few minutes and in between making a beautiful laugh again and again. And this scenario brings tears of happiness in the eyes of Suraj mother.

Finally after a week Dalip Singh was discharged from the hospital and all family members' leaves for their home thanking everyone for their valuable help. The ACP sends the police van to take them all to their village.

CHAPTER FIVE

A NIGHT IN THE ROOM

Abid Ali hails from a small town and was a very hardworking young boy of 23 years. He was highly educated, but he belongs to a poor family which consists of 9 members. He was very responsible person in the family. He always wants to do something special for his family so that his family members could have a decent and peaceful life. After completion of studies he starts appearing in competitive exams in search of government jobs. And soon he was rewarded by Almighty for his hard work and got job in revenue department and was appointed on junior assistant post. His first place posting was a beautiful and small town of Bhadurpur. Abid initially after joining the duties got accommodation in men working hostel in the first year. In this is very hard to find independent accommodation of 1 BHK. But Abid keeps trying for this continuously and after his sincere after he got the desired accommodation in the town. The main reason of trying for independent accommodation was that he was preparing for administrative examination.

The 1 BHK accommodations was situated in corner side locality of the town in whose adjoining area was a dense jungle. It was also near to his office with basic amenities available nearby. Here his major of clothes washing was also solved as a laundry shop situated in the vicinity of his accommodation. The owner of that laundry shop was a noble person and provided services to Abid at a economical rate. With the passage of time Abid got familiar with many people but laundry shop owner was the closest person to him. The laundry owner also helps him many ways. One way of his help was he asks Abid to everyday to his shop for spending some time. As he made very clear to him that it is very hard to spent ideal time for any person who is new to the place. On shop mother of owner who was aged about 81 years use to sit outside the shop on a bench. Soon Abid get well versed that old lady and both starts to enjoy each other company. Now Abid was able to spend his ideal time here regularly. It has passed nearly 6 months of Abid residing in this locality.

It was a nice cool evening after a rain shower when Abid returns to his room after having dinner outside. He after reaching his room just lay down on the bed with a light blanket and was listening to the music. He was planning to do some studies after a short spell of relaxation. But soon he felt sleep and he wakes up around 1.10 AM , When he wake first he see the time in the clock and pick a water bottle which he always kept near his bed for drinking water, Though he was also feeling pressure for urination at that time. As he was drinking the water he just felt that some is standing outside his room window and peeping in. Firstly he just overlooked it, but after a while he realizes that surely someone is standing outside room window. So just walk very slowly and carefully at close to the edge of window and see outside, where he show that a person who was taller than his window height which was 7 feet and had a big ugly face plus his eyes were burning red was standing. He was seeing into the room and also making an awkward sound, which very horrifying. At this moment Abid got so scared that he starts sweating in that very cold climate at that time.

After watching for next few minutes he just put off the light of the room and lay down on the bed again with his eyes closed just starts chanting religious mantras. At this his urge for urination was very high, but due to his fear and situation he cannot go outside for urination at that point. He keeps on chanting the mantras for Almighty help at that moment. After sometime he sleeps in the state of his fear. When he wake up it was 5.20 AM and the sunlight has just started to spread, but still make sure that the man he shows was not standing outside his room window. And when he got assured he just ran outside and urinates. But due to long control of urination urge a severe pain arises in his urine bladder. And thus he has to the hospital immediately. Where he was given a injection and prescribed to take medicines for next seven days. The negative effect of witnessing which might be some evil spirit starts happening in Abid life from the moment onwards. For the next 10 days he faced many happening with himself. He even on two or three had some narrow escapes. These all unexpected happening makes Abid very fearful. But he was not getting any clue at this moment. He starts getting very depressed which many people noticed.

And it had passed exactly fifteen days when one day he visited the laundry shop. He met old at the entrance of shop who seeing him immediately ask him – why he was looking depressed. And where was he for last fifteen days. Is everything is okay. On this Abid replied – its okay. But old lady at once ask him another question and making him sit alongside. Please whether he faces any supernatural incidence in the accommodation in which he is residing. On this question Abid goes silent. But after a while – he said how she knew that. On this old said I am over 80 years of age and very much familiar with surroundings and happenings. She can even read faces and mental condition of people. On asking this he told each and everything which happened with on that night and thereafter. The old lady after listening to Abid told him that she wants to tell reality of that part of place in which you resides. That corner place is known to be haunted place as an evil spirit cast his shadow there. Many supernatural happening have been reported to happen in that place with people. I myself also faced one such supernatural happening when my son was too small. But as you very young I cannot explain it to you at this moment.

After listening to this Abid got scared and noticing this old lady asks him to stay in there instead of staying there and advised him to find new accommodation immediately. So Abid starts living with laundry shop owner from that day onwards. And just after 8 days he got government accommodation which was situated about 3 kilometers from that area. But the help provided by old lady and her family makes a deep impression in the heart of Abid. And as a result between them a close and friendly relationship develops from those days onwards forever. The office is close to that laundry shop and Abid still met old lady and her son regularly.

But that supernatural happening had cast a permanent impression on Abid. Still whenever he crosses area of that house, a sense of fear just erupts in his mind.

www.ingramcontent.com/pod-product-compliance
Lightning Source LLC
Chambersburg PA
CBHW061408160726
47995CB00002B/513